Little Brother

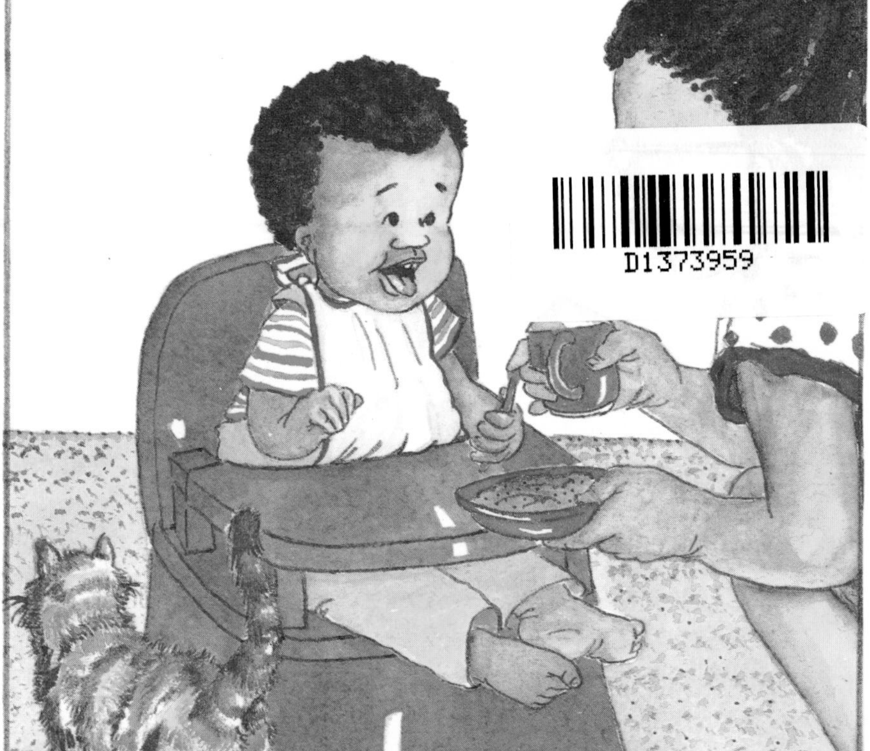

Story by Joy Cowley

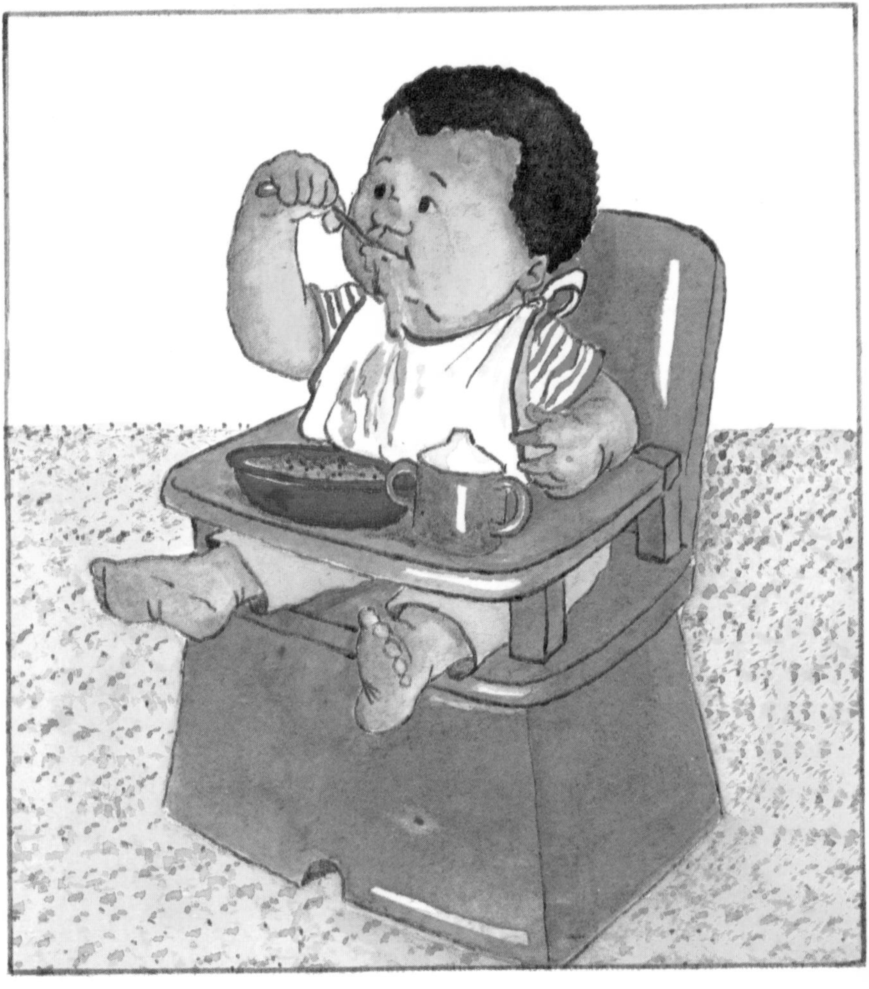

He eats,

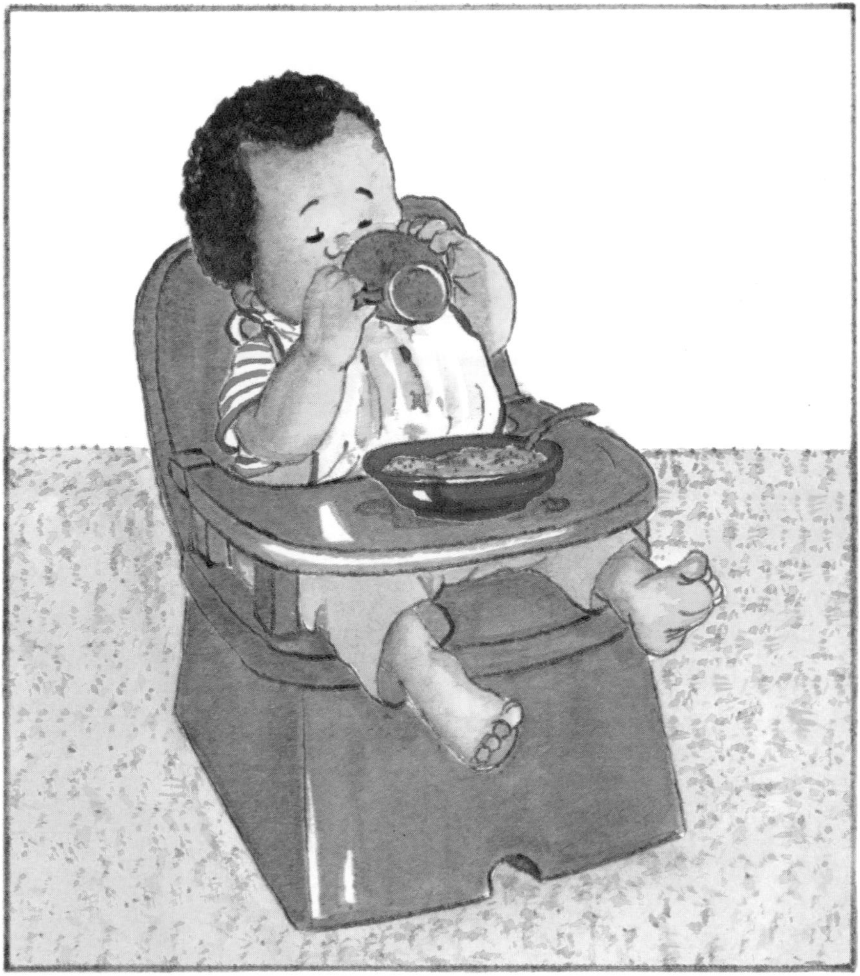

he drinks,

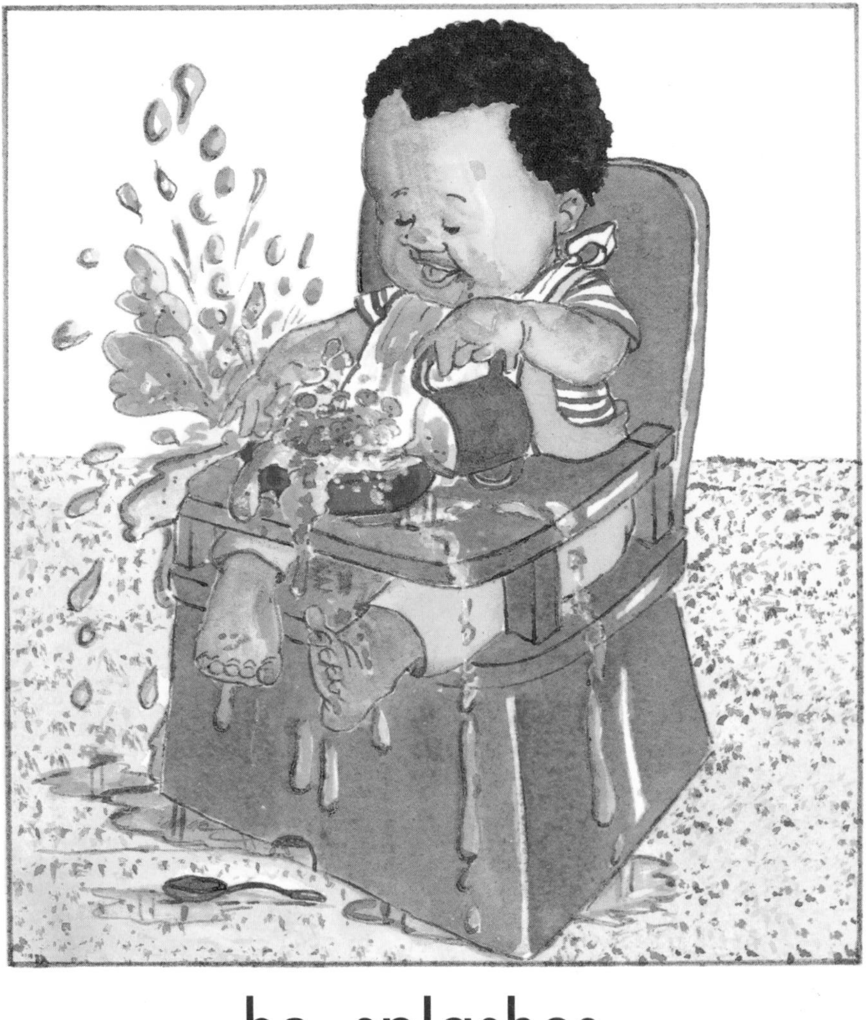

he splashes,

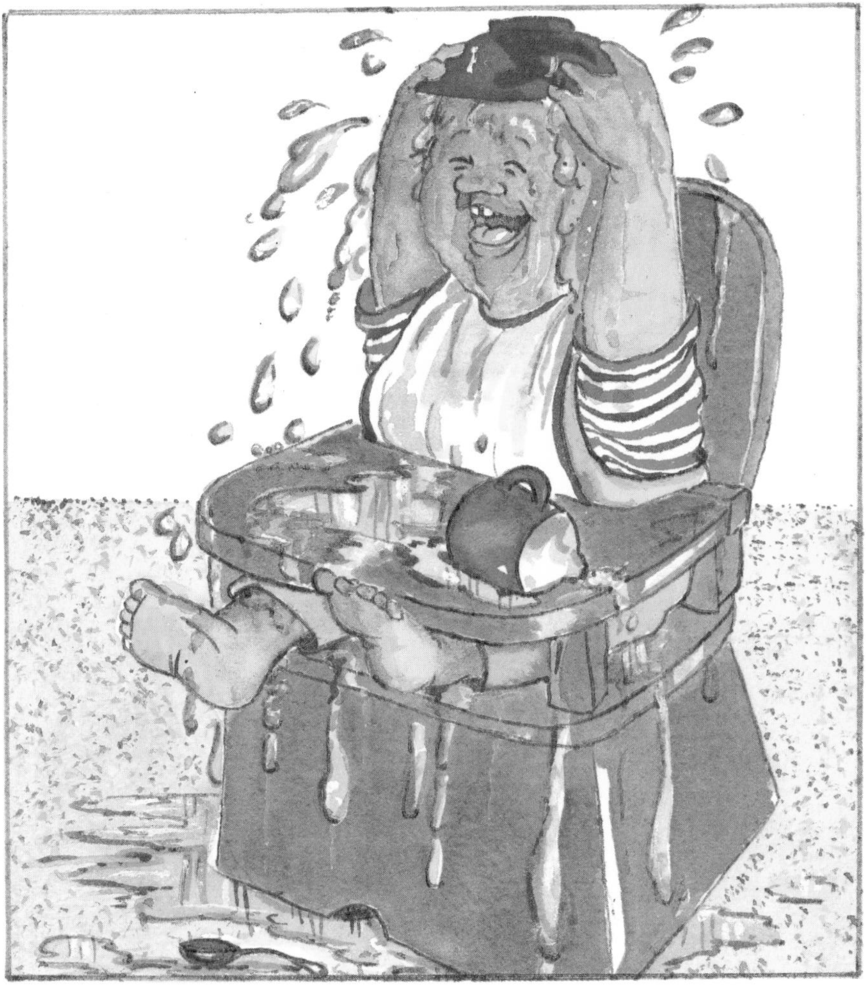

he laughs,

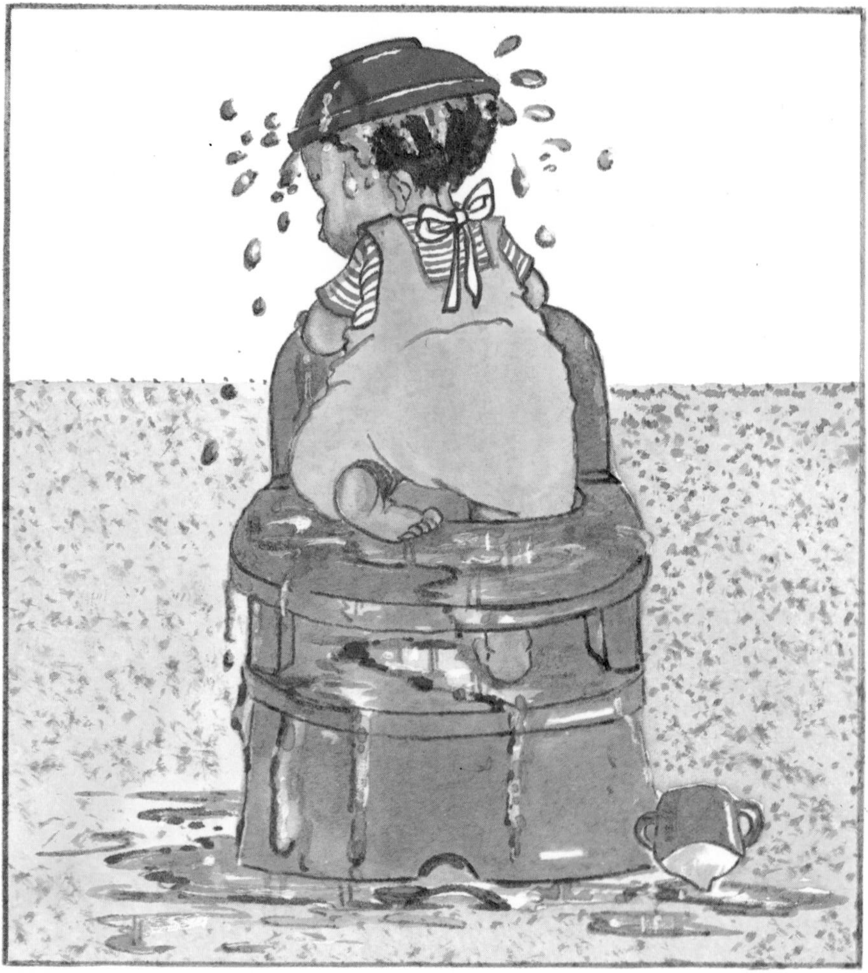

he climbs,

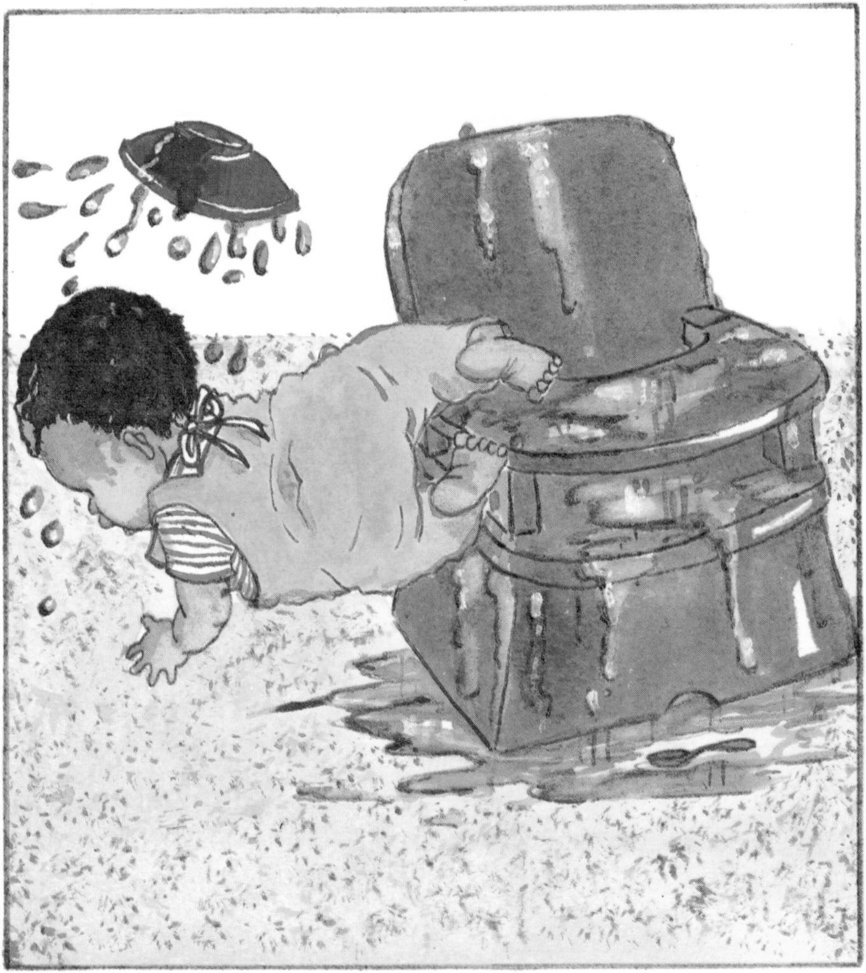

he falls,

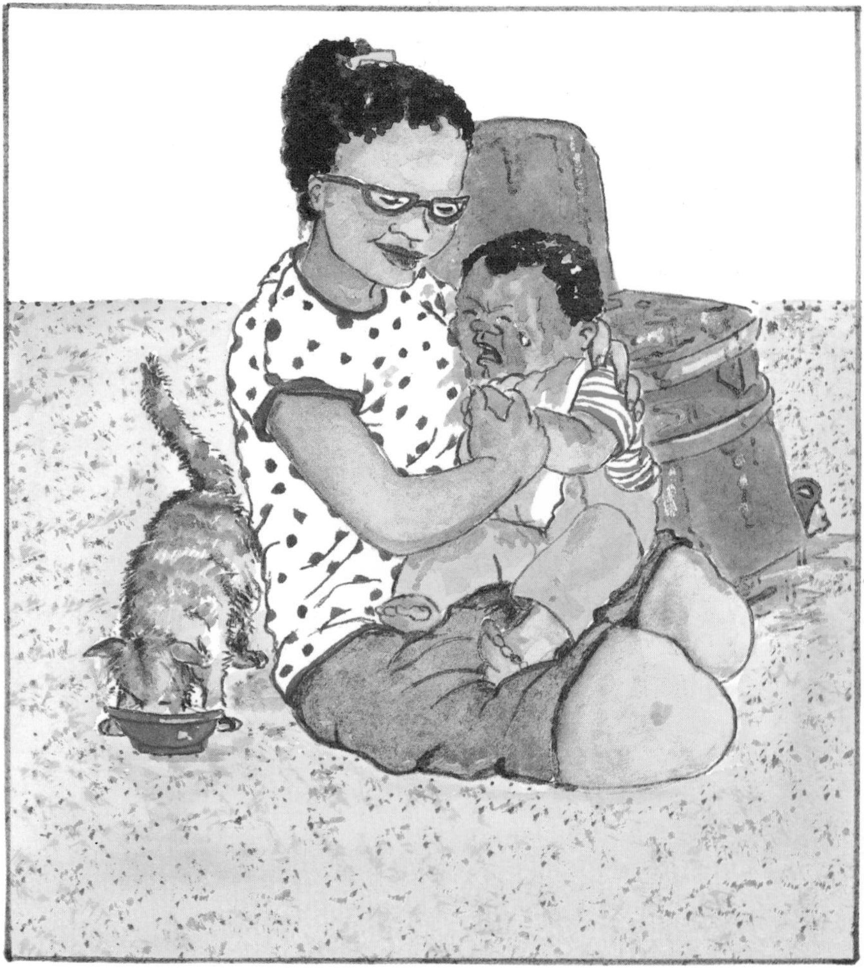

he cries.